Indian Two Feet and His Horse

By MARGARET FRISKEY

Pictures by EZRA JACK KEATS

SCHOLASTIC INC.

New York Toronto London Auckland Sydney

ISBN 0-590-42429-7

Copyright © 1959 by Childrens Press. Copyright © 1964 by Scholastic Inc. This edition published by Scholastic Inc., 730 Broadway, New York, N.Y. 10003, by arrangement with Childrens Press.

12 11 10 9 8 7 6 5 4 3 2 1   8 9/8 0 1 2 3/9

Printed in the U.S.A.   08

There was
a little Indian.
He wished
he had a horse.

But he did not
have a horse.

He had to walk, walk, walk.

He could sing.

He could dance.

He could skin a deer
for hide. But he could
not ride a horse.

He had to walk.

He could listen to a story.

He could paint
with a piece of bone.
But he had no horse.
He *wished* he had a horse.

He walked
to the woods.

He walked
to the river.

He walked to the top of a high, high hill.

Oh, how he
wished he had a horse!

He could ride down
the hill on a rock.

He could ride a big, fat log.

He could swing
across a river
from a tree.
But, of course,
he could not ride
a horse.

He did not have one.

"Little Two Feet,"
said his father.

"You must think like a horse to find one.
Go find one."

Little Two Feet
walked to some
tall grass.

"If I were a horse,"
said Two Feet,
"I would put my nose
into this grass."

But he did not find
a horse.

He ran to a river.

"If I were a horse,"
said Two Feet, "I would
put my nose into this river."

But he did not find a horse.

He ran to a hill
where the sun was hot.
"If I were a horse,"
said Two Feet, "I would
find a cool, cool spot."

So he sat
in the shadow
of a big, old rock,
and he went to sleep.

Did he find a horse? No.
He didn't find a horse. But—

. . . a horse found him.

Now a horse
has four feet,
but this one
stood on three.
He held up a
sore foot for
Two Feet to see.

"Oh," said Two Feet.
"If I were a horse
with one bad foot,
I would need some help
from a boy like me."

Two Feet put
his shirt around
his horse's leg,
to help him hold
his sore foot
off the ground.

"I will help you,"
said Two Feet.
"Come with me."

Little Two Feet
had a horse. But
he still had to walk!

They came
to a river.
And they
both had a drink.

They came to the grass
so long and cool.

They rested for a while.

And then they walked some more.

And at last
they both came home.
"Little Two Feet
has a horse!" said
his father.

And they all danced and sang.

Every day, Two Feet
brought his horse
some water.

He brought him
some grass.

He took care of
that horse's foot
until the foot
was well.

And then he *rode*
to the woods.

He *rode* to the river.

He *rode* to the top of a high, high hill.

He had a horse!